Gwen Logan.

D1633962

Gwen Logan.

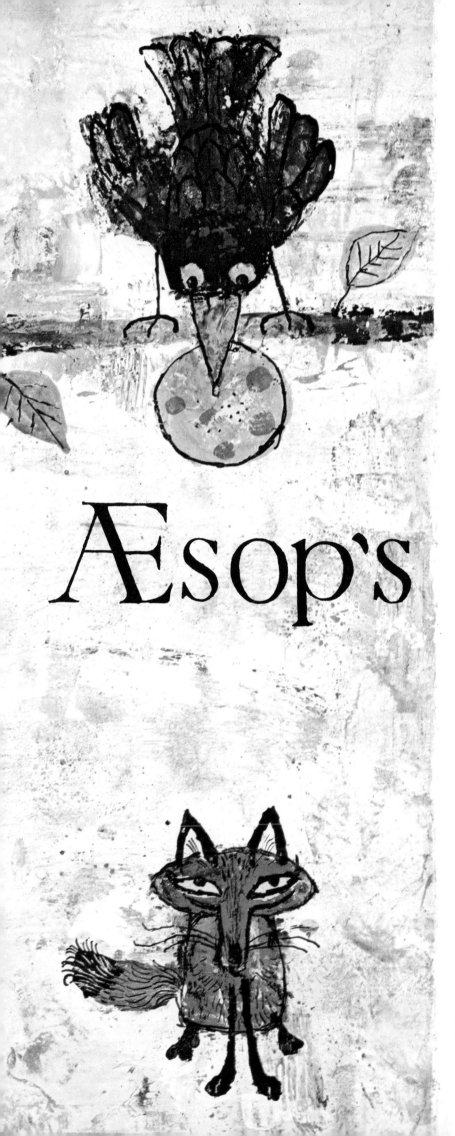

Æsop's Fables

SELECTED AND ADAPTED
BY LOUIS UNTERMEYER

ILLUSTRATED BY
A. and M. PROVENSEN

PAUL HAMLYN • LONDON

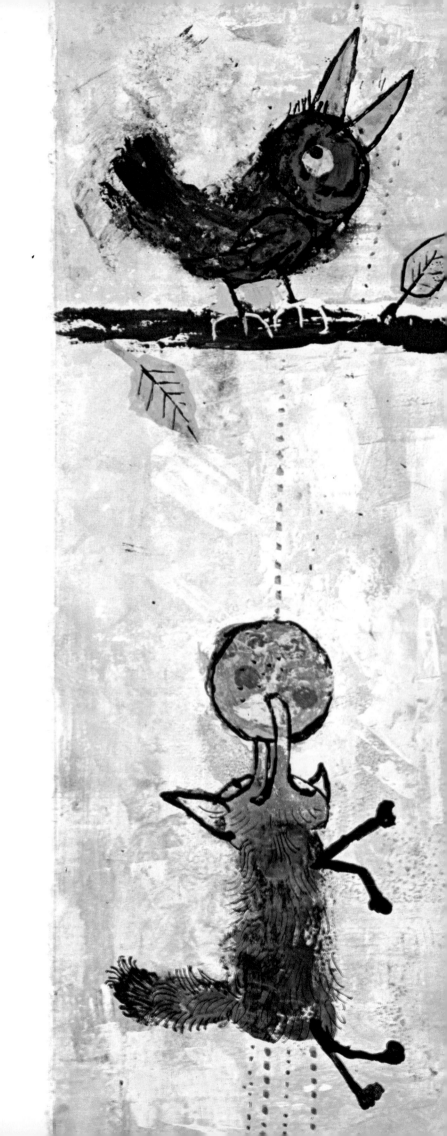

PUBLISHED 1965 BY PAUL HAMLYN, LTD.,
WESTBOOK HOUSE, FULHAM BROADWAY, LONDON
FOR GOLDEN PLEASURE BOOKS LTD.
© 1965 BY GOLDEN PRESS, INC. ALL RIGHTS RESERVED.
PRINTED IN THE U.S.A.

TABLE OF CONTENTS

A Foreword	9
The Gnat on the Bull's Horn	10
The Grasshopper and the Ant	12
The Lioness and the Vixen	13
The Rooster and the Jewel	16
The Boy and the Wolf	17
The Lion's Share	20
The Mice and the Cat on the Wall	22
The Fox and the Grapes	23
The Lion, the Boar, and the Vultures	26
The Cat and the Mice	27
The Travellers and the Bear	30
The Ass in the Lion's Skin	32
The Goose and the Golden Eggs	33
The Mice and the Weasels	36
The Dog and the Shadow	37
The Eagle and the Tortoise	41
The Frogs Who Asked for a King	42
The Dog in the Manger	43
Venus and the Lovesick Cat	46
The Jackdaw's Fine Feathers	47
The Hungry Wolf and the Lamb	50
The Strong Bundle of Sticks	52
The Country Maid and the Milk Pail	53
The Lion and the Mouse	56
The Town Mouse and the Country Mouse	57
The Fox and the Crow	60
The Oak and the Reed	62
The Strength of Wind and Sun	63
The Nurse and the Wolf	66
The Crow and the Pitcher	67
The Boastful Bullfrog and the Bull	70
The Lions and the Hares	71
The Cunning Cat and His Company	74
The Wolf in Sheep's Clothing	76
The Great and Little Fishes	77
The Hungry Old Lion and the Wise Fox	80
The Fox and the Mask	82
The Hare and the Tortoise	83
The Tricky Fox and the Stork	86
The Miller, the Son, and the Donkey	87

A FOREWORD

WE KNOW LITTLE about Aesop the man or the author. We cannot be certain when and where he was born, how he lived, and when he died. He is presumed to have lived in the sixth or seventh century B.C., but accounts of his life did not appear until almost two thousand years later. The descriptions were so different that some scholars believe Aesop never existed and that his works were the product of several story-tellers rather than one man.

According to the favourite version Aesop was born some twenty-five hundred years ago

in Asia Minor. He was, says one writer, an undersized, bow-legged, ugly little fellow with a head too big for his body. However, another writer says nothing about any unpleasant features. On the contrary, he claims that a noble statue was set up by the Athenians in memory of Aesop, and "noble" is not a word which would have been used about a deformed person. It is conceded that he was a servant, quick-witted, always ready to entertain and, at the same time, able to instruct. After finding

his way to the court of Croesus, he was sent to many places on the king's business. He served his master not only as a story-teller but as a diplomat. Since he did not want to offend people by referring to their faults, he told about the sly plots and tricky schemes of men but he made it seem they were the thoughts and words of animals. He did this so cleverly that it was sometimes hard to tell whether it was a human being or an animal that was scheming and talking.

All of Aesop's stories, or fables, contained lessons for his listeners. Sometimes the idea was plain enough in the telling; sometimes a moral was added to point the lesson. When the Athenians complained that they were tired of being ruled by a certain monarch, Aesop told them the fable of "The Frogs Who Asked for a King." When the citizens of Delphi greedily demanded more money than Aesop had brought, he related the story of "The Goose and the Golden Eggs."

Aesop did not invent all his stories. Some of them had been heard long before his time in Egypt and Babylon. But Aesop gave the tales his own personal touch. He told—or retold—the stories so simply, so wisely and so winningly, that they have been enjoyed for thousands of years not only by scholars and teachers but by children all over the world.

Aesop never wrote his fables. He told them wherever he went, and his listeners retold them; the fables travelled by word of mouth from one country to another. Later, when they were written down, some of them appeared in verse; most of them, however, were printed in prose. But whatever form the fables took, they lost none of their wisdom or their charm. The lessons they teach are as true for us today as they were for the ancients. The humour and humanity of the fables keep them —and will continue to keep them—happily alive, as lively as they are lasting.

The Gnat on the Bull's Horn

A Gnat had been buzzing about the field all day. Toward evening he grew tired and looked about for a place to rest. He found it on the horn of a Bull who was eating grass. After he had sat there for some time, he spoke to the Bull.

"Sir," said the Gnat, "I don't want to be a burden. If my weight bothers you, say so, and I'll fly away."

"Do as you like," snorted the Bull. "I didn't feel you when you came, and I won't miss you when you're gone."

Sometimes the smallest people have the biggest opinion of themselves.

The Grasshopper and the Ant

One clear winter's day an Ant dragged out some grains of food to dry in the sun. A hungry Grasshopper passing by asked the Ant to let him have some of the food.

"Why do you come to me to be fed?" asked the Ant. "What were you doing during the summer?"

"Oh," replied the Grasshopper, "I spent the summer singing."

"Well, then," said the Ant, "you sang all summer, you can dance all winter."

You can't play all the time.

The Lioness and the Vixen

All the animals were boasting about their large families. Only the Lioness kept silent. She did not utter a word, even when a Vixen paraded her brood in front of the Lioness.

"Look!" said the Vixen. "Look at my litter of red foxes—seven of them! Tell me, how many do *you* have at a birth?"

"Only one," replied the Lioness quietly. "But that one is a Lion!"

It's quality that counts, not quantity.

The Rooster and the Jewel

A hungry Rooster was scratching for food in the barnyard when he saw a jewel gleaming in the straw. He seized upon it as if it were a piece of corn, but he could neither crack it nor swallow it. Dropping it, he said, "You are a very fine thing without a doubt; you shine in the straw and I suppose you are very valuable. But you are not to my taste. I would give you and all the jewels in the world for one good barley-corn."

Every man to his own taste, or,
a thing is good only if it is good for you.

The Boy and the Wolf

A Boy who was employed to tend sheep was often bored with the task. To create a little excitement he would rush toward the village crying, "Wolf! Wolf!" When the villagers came with clubs and pitchforks to help him, they found nothing. This seemed such a good sport that a few days later the Boy cried out again, and once more the people ran to help him.

One day a Wolf actually did come out of the forest. But this time when the Boy cried, "Wolf! Wolf!" the villagers thought he was playing his tricks again, and refused to stir. Meanwhile the sheep were at the mercy of the Wolf, who enjoyed a hearty meal.

A liar will not be believed
even when he speaks the truth.

That was fun. I'll do it again...

...and again,

The Lion's Share

There had been much fighting among the beasts of prey. They could not agree whether one animal was entitled to more food than another. Finally they decided that everything should be shared.

One day, a Lion, a Tiger, a Leopard and a Jackal went hunting together. They caught a plump deer and it was divided into four equal parts. Since the Lion was king, he was the one who gave out the portions.

"The first piece," said the Lion, "is for me because I am the Lion. The second piece is for the bravest, and that's me again. The third piece is for the strongest, and there's no doubt that I am stronger than any of you. As for the fourth piece— I dare anyone to touch it!"

Some people believe that Might makes Right.

What a Bully!

The Mice and the Cat on the Wall

The house in the country had stood empty for years. Then the Field Mice moved in. After a while there were so many of them that they filled every nook, corner, crack and cranny of the house.

A Cat heard about this and moved in, too. She never had to leave the house to hunt. She had Mice for breakfast, lunch, dinner, and also, when she felt like it, for afternoon tea.

The Mice became alarmed. Their numbers grew less every day.

"Something must be done," said one of the Mice.

"But what?" said another. "That Cat is much too big for us to fight."

"The best attack is defence," said the oldest Mouse. "We will stay in our holes until the Cat gets hungry and goes away."

The Cat waited for hours and hours. But not a Mouse showed as much as a whisker. After three days the Cat decided she would trick them into coming out of their holes so that she could get at them again. She climbed up the wall, tied her back legs together, and hung herself head down from a nail. She did not make a sound.

"Come on out," said one of the young Mice. "It's safe now. The Cat's dead." But the old Mouse shook his head. He poked his head a half-inch out of the hole and called.

"It's no use, Cat," he said. "You may pretend you're dead, but we know better. We wouldn't trust you if you were hanging up there in a sack. We will not come out as long as you are here."

The Cat did not wait any longer. She untied herself, came down and, with an angry whine, went away.

Once bitten, twice shy.

The Fox and the Grapes

The Fox had gone without breakfast as well as without dinner, so when he found himself in a vineyard his mouth began to water. There was one particularly juicy-looking bunch of grapes hanging on a trellis. The Fox leaped to pull it down, but it was just beyond his reach. He went back a few steps, took a running start, and jumped again. Again he missed. Once more he tried, and once more he failed to get the tempting prize. Finally, weary and worn out, he left the vineyard. "I really wasn't very hungry," he said, to console himself. "Besides, I'm sure those grapes are sour."

There is comfort in pretending that what we can't get isn't worth having.

The Lion, the Boar, and the Vultures

It was the hottest day of the summer. The rivers had shrunk; streams had gone underground; springs had dried up. All the animals were suffering from the heat. They roamed about unhappily, trying to find water.

Suddenly a Lion spied a small pool half-hidden in a shady grove. At the same time a Boar saw it, too. Both of them ran to satisfy their thirst.

"Keep away!" growled the Lion. "I am your king, and you must wait until I'm finished."

"You may call yourself king," said the Boar, "but you are a bully. It's a small pool, and if I let you drink first, you would drink every drop."

"Don't you dare talk back to me!" roared the Lion. "Do as I tell you! Off with you!"

"Here I stay," said the Boar between his teeth. "It's my pool as much as it is yours. If you want it, you'll have to fight for it."

So they fought. The Lion leaped, spreading his huge claws like twenty daggers. But the Boar sprang to one side and escaped with nothing worse than deep slashes. Then the Boar charged, using his two sharp tusks, and tore some of the Lion's hide. The struggle grew fierce. The wounds grew worse; both animals were covered with blood. Pausing a moment to catch his breath, the Lion happened to look up. Circling above, he saw a flock of vultures, birds of death who feed on dead bodies.

"Look!" said the Lion. "Vultures! They're waiting—waiting for one of us, or both, to be killed. Let us stop this foolish fighting. Better be friends than become food for others. Come, let us drink together."

In a false quarrel there is no true valour.

The Cat and the Mice

The Mice were much bothered by a Cat. They decided to hold a council to see what could be done about the matter. During the meeting a young mouse there said, "If the Cat had a little bell tied to her neck, it would tinkle every time she made a step. This would warn us, and we would have plenty of time to reach our homes in safety."

All the Mice applauded this clever scheme until one of them spoke up and said, "It's a fine plan. But which one of us is going to put the bell on the Cat?"

*It is easier to think up a plan
than to carry it out.*

The Travellers and the Bear

One evening two travellers were walking through the woods. It was dark, and the first traveller said, "I don't like the looks of this place. But there are two of us. We are friends, and if we stick together nothing can harm us."

At that moment a Bear suddenly appeared.

The first traveller yelled and, without a thought for his friend, sprang up a tree. The second traveller, left alone and knowing he had no chance single-handed against the Bear, threw himself down on the ground. He lay flat, not moving a muscle and scarcely breathing. Someone had told him that a Bear will not touch dead meat.

The Bear ambled up to the second traveller, sniffed at him, nuzzled his head, then snuffed at his nose, mouth and ears. The man never moved. His body was stiff; he held his breath. After a few minutes, the Bear, thinking the man was dead, gave a low growl and shuffled off.

When the Bear had gone, the first traveller came down from the tree.

"Well," he said, laughing, "I noticed that the Bear put his mouth close to your ear. What did he tell you?"

"He told me the truth," said the second traveller. "He told me never to trust anyone who says he will stand by you, and then runs away as soon as there is trouble."

A friend in need is a friend in deed.

The Ass in the Lion's Skin

An Ass once found the skin of a dead Lion. Putting it on, he frightened all the animals by strutting about without a sound. Only the clever Fox was suspicious. In an attempt to frighten him, the Ass tried to roar. As soon as he heard the familiar bray, the Fox laughed and said, "I, too, might have been alarmed if you had kept your mouth shut."

Clothes do not make the man.
Your talk gives you away.

The Goose and the Golden Eggs

A Man had the great good fortune to own a marvellous Goose —every day it laid a golden egg. The Man was growing rich, but the more he got, the more he wanted. Making up his mind to have the whole treasure at once, he killed the Goose. But when he killed her and cut her open, instead of finding a horde of golden eggs, he found that she was just like any other Goose.

Beware of being greedy.
It doesn't pay to be impatient.

The Mice and the Weasels

The war between the Mice and the Weasels had been going on for a long time. The Mice were losing every battle and, after one more defeat, they called a meeting to discuss the situation.

"The trouble is we are poorly organized," said one Mouse.

"The trouble is the Weasels don't fight fair," said another.

"The real trouble," said a third Mouse, "is that nobody is in command of our scattered army. What we need is leaders."

Before the meeting broke up, the Mice had chosen several leaders, and these were named generals. The generals were proud of their position; they insisted on wearing decorations that would show their rank. Besides putting medals on their chests, they placed large, gilded horns on their heads.

All went well until the next battle. The Weasels won again and the Mice had to retreat. Most of them were lucky to escape into their holes. But when the generals tried to follow the other Mice, they could not get into the holes because of their fancy horns. The Weasels caught them easily and ate every one.

Vanity costs more than it's worth.

The Dog and the Shadow

A Dog who had stolen a large bone was carrying it off in order to enjoy his meal without interference. Crossing a bridge he happened to see his shadow in the unrippled pool. He thought it was another Dog with another large bone and, to his greedy eyes, the other bone looked larger than his. He snarled and made a grab for the other Dog's bone—whereupon he dropped his own. The bone fell into the water, sank, and was lost, and the Dog slunk away hungrier than ever.

The greedy man cheats himself, or, when you grasp at the shadow you lose the substance.

The Eagle and the Tortoise

A Tortoise was not satisfied with his life. He wanted to stop being a Tortoise.

"I'm tired of crawling along, inch by inch, foot after foot, getting nowhere in particular," he grumbled. "I want to be able to skim and dive and float in the air."

He spoke to the Eagle about it. The Eagle tried to discourage him.

"You're not built for flying," the Eagle told the Tortoise.

"Don't worry about that," answered the Tortoise. "I've watched how the birds do it. Even if I haven't got wings, I can make my four flippers act like four stout oars in the air the way I do in the water. Just get me up there, and you'll see I can fly as well as any of the birds. Besides, if you'll carry me as high as the clouds I'll bring you lots of rare pearls from the sea."

The Eagle was tempted, and carried the Tortoise up to a great height. "Now, then," cried the Eagle, "fly!"

But the moment the Tortoise was on his own, he fell from the sky. He fell like a stone, and on a stone he landed. He struck with such force that he was smashed into little pieces.

Be satisfied with what and where you are.
The higher you fly the harder you may fall.

The Frogs Who Asked for a King

The Frogs who lived at liberty in a lake grew tired of their freedom. They sent a petition to Jupiter asking for a ruler. The great god smiled, and threw a log into the lake. The Frogs were awed by the splash it made. They clustered around the log in worship.

Soon, however, they discovered that the log was a lifeless thing, something which could not inspire either their faith or their fear. Again they petitioned Jupiter, pleading for a more potent and powerful king.

This time Jupiter sent down a stork, whose favourite food happened to be Frogs. Within a few hours the Frogs had lost not only their freedom but their lives as well.

Be content with what you have.

The Dog in the Manger

A Dog decided to make his home on a pile of hay that lay in a Cow's manger. He was asleep when the Cow came into the barnyard for her evening meal.

"Please," said the Cow, who was very polite, "get down. That's my food you're lying on."

"Go away!" snarled the Dog. "Can't you see I'm sleeping here?"

"But it's my food," the Cow repeated.

"Yes," added a Donkey who had followed the Cow. "You don't eat hay, and we do."

"We need it," said a Ram who had followed the Donkey. "Hay is for the hungry."

But the Dog would not let any of the animals get to the manger. He barked and bellowed and tried to bite them when they came too near. Finally, he made so much noise that they had to leave.

Don't keep those who need something
from getting what you don't need.

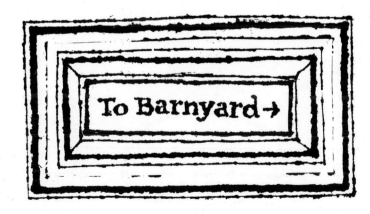

Venus and the Lovesick Cat

No matter how other things may be changed, can anyone or anything change its nature?

Long, long ago in ancient Greece, a cat fell in love with a young man. The cat lived in the temple of Venus, and she prayed to the goddess to change her into a girl. Venus took pity on the lovesick creature and turned her into a beautiful maiden. As soon as the young man saw her he, too, fell in love.

"You are the most exquisite thing my eyes have ever looked upon," he told her. "I know I am not worthy of you, but will you let me hope that someday you may be my wife?"

The day came soon, and they were married. She was not only beautiful, but a devoted bride. She was an excellent housekeeper, an accomplished cook, and the most affectionate of wives.

Venus was proud of her. But she could not help wondering whether her character had changed. One night when the husband was away, she determined to find out. She sent a mouse into the bedroom.

The moment the girl saw the mouse, she jumped out of bed. She did not scream as women are supposed to do. Instead, she leaped across the room, pounced, and seized the mouse in her teeth. She shook it until it was dead, and then calmly went back to bed.

We can change everything except our nature.

The Jackdaw's Fine Feathers

A Jackdaw, a plain black bird a little smaller than a crow, fancied himself too good for his companions.

"They say that clothes make the man," he told himself. "I must stop going around in this dull black outfit."

Finding some bright feathers that a peacock had shed, he stuck them all over himself.

"Now," said the Jackdaw, "I am well dressed. All the birds will have to admire me." And he strutted like a peacock across the lawn.

But the birds were not deceived. They mocked him and, when he continued to parade in his borrowed plumes, pecked at him until all the fine feathers were torn off.

"I must have made a mistake," he said ruefully. "I ought to go back and stay with my own kind."

But his own kind would have none of him. The other Jackdaws refused to let him join the flock. "You have given yourself too many airs," they said. "We were not good enough for you yesterday; now you are not good enough for us."

Be yourself. Fine feathers do not always make fine birds.

How beautiful I am!

How elegant!

Beauty is only skin deep.

The Hungry Wolf and the Lamb

A Wolf was drinking from a river when he happened to raise his head from the stream. Lower down he spied a Lamb lapping up a little water.

"Oho!" said the Wolf to himself. "There's my supper! All I need is a good excuse to get it. Then I will have both my food and my drink together."

"You there!" he growled. "What do you mean by muddying my water!"

"I'm sorry," said the Lamb. "But I can't be muddying the water. If your water is muddy it's not my fault. See, I'm using only the tip of my tongue. Besides, I'm drinking downstream from you, and I couldn't possibly disturb the water further up where you are."

"Don't argue with me!" snarled the Wolf. "I know all about you! You've been going around for over six months saying nasty things about me."

"That can't be," the Lamb bleated. "I was born only three months ago."

"Well," snapped the Wolf, "if it wasn't you, it was your father. That's just as bad."

And, before the Lamb could say another word, the Wolf sprang on the poor creature and ate her up.

A bad excuse is good enough for a bully.

The Strong Bundle of Sticks

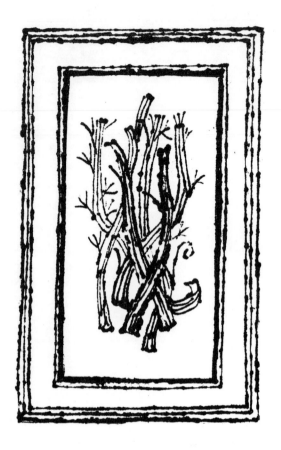

An old farmer felt he was near death. He was sad to leave his farm and his family. But what made him sadder was that his three sons were always quarrelling. He had often told them how important it was that they should live together in peace. But they did not listen. As he lay on his bed, he asked the oldest to bring him a bundle of sticks.

He had the young man tie the bundle together. "Now," he said. "Break that bundle."

The oldest tried, but he could not do it. The second son tried, and he, too, failed. The third son did no better. The bundle could not be broken.

"Untie it," said the father. "Now see if you can break one of the separate sticks."

The oldest son broke the stick without any effort. The second son took another stick and broke it easily. So did the third son.

"You see now," said the father, with a smile on his face, "why it is important to stop quarrelling and stick together. As long as you separate yourselves from each other you will be weak. United, you will be so strong that no one can hurt you."

In union there is strength. Divided we fall;
united we stand.

The Country Maid and the Milk Pail

Peggy was a milkmaid. A country girl, she had learned to carry things on her head. And this day on her head she was carrying a pail of milk to the market.

"Let me see," she thought as she walked along the road, "I shall sell this pail of milk for a good bit of money. With the money I shall buy three dozen eggs. I shall then put the eggs under our old hen and wait until they are all hatched. Soon I shall have a whole yardful of young chickens and, though a few of them may die, there should be plenty to fetch a good price. I shall wait until winter when poultry is more expensive, and then I shall get enough money for the chickens to buy myself a new dress. Maybe there will be enough left over to get a jacket and a hat with ribbons. I'll have them all in a matching colour—yellow, perhaps, or green—everyone says I look lovely in green—or maybe blue—blue really is my colour on account of my blue eyes—although sometimes I think pink suits me best. Anyway, I'll have a beautiful new outfit for the fair. All the boys will want to dance with me and all the girls will be jealous. But I don't care. I'll just toss my head—like this!"

That's just what she did. She gave her head such a toss that the pail fell off and all the milk was spilled. Goodbye now to the eggs and chickens and dress and jacket and the hat with ribbons. Goodbye to the fair and the dancing boys and the jealous girls. Goodbye to those lovely daydreams. Alas.

Don't count your chickens until they're hatched.

Milk Money equals Egg Money equals Chicken Money equals

When my dreams come true..

..How beautiful I'll be.

The Lion and the Mouse

One day a Mouse happened to run over the paws of a sleeping Lion. Angrily the mighty beast woke and seized the offender. He was about to crush the little animal when the Mouse cried out, "Please, mighty monarch, spare me. I would be only a tiny mouthful, and you would not relish me. Besides, I might be able to help you some day. You never can tell."

The idea that this insignificant creature could ever help him amused the Lion so much that he let his little prisoner go.

Some time after this the Lion, roaming the forest for food, was caught in a hunter's net. The more he struggled the more he became entangled; his roar of rage echoed through the forest. Hearing the sound, the Mouse ran to the trap and began to gnaw the ropes that bound the Lion. It was not long before he had severed the last cord with his little teeth and set the huge beast free.

Don't belittle little things.

The Town Mouse and the Country Mouse

One day the country Mouse invited his friend, the city Mouse, to visit him. The country Mouse put out the best that he had in his pantry—kernels of corn and barley seeds, acorns and nuts, wild berries and sweet-tasting flower stalks. But the town Mouse turned up his nose. "How can you eat such stuff!" he complained. "And how can you live in such a hole! No fun, no excitement; nothing to do from one day to another. Come with me. Let me show you some of the pleasures and sights of the city."

It was a large house to which they came; the country Mouse was struck with its size and splendour. "We will explore it all in the morning," said the town Mouse proudly. "Tonight we will take it easy. Wait until you see the banquet I've made ready for us!"

It was dark when they crept softly into the kitchen. Everyone had gone to bed, but there were still remains of a lavish dinner. There were remnants of cake, bacon rinds, parings of rich cheese, potato peelings, butter to lick, and wine left in the glasses. The country Mouse was in raptures.

Just as they began to enjoy their feast, something terrible descended on them. It was the house-cat who sprang with bared teeth and unsheathed claws through the door. They were lucky to escape into a cranny.

"Goodbye," said the country Mouse the next morning. "You have a beautiful house and wonderful food, but I prefer my dried seeds and my quiet hole in the ground."

A crust with comfort is better than a feast with fear.

The Fox and the Crow

A Crow had stolen a good-sized piece of cheese from a cottage window and had flown with it into a tall tree. A Fox, who had seen this happen, said to himself, "If I am smart, I will have cheese for supper tonight." He thought for a moment, and then decided on this plan.

"Good afternoon, Miss Crow," he said. "How really beautiful you look today. I've never seen your feathers so glistening. Your neck is as graceful as a swan's and your wings are mightier than an eagle's. I am sure that if you had a voice, you would sing as sweetly as a nightingale."

The Crow, pleased with such praise, wanted to prove that she could sing. As soon as she opened her mouth to caw, the cheese fell to the ground and the Fox snapped it up.

As he trotted off he made things worse by calling back to the Crow, "I may have talked much about your beauty, but I said nothing about your brains."

Don't be fooled by flattery.

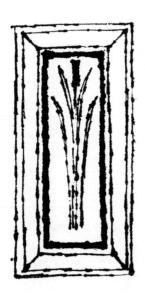

The Oak and the Reed

An Oak tree and a Reed grew side by side on the brim of a river. From time to time they spoke to each other, but they were not good friends. The mighty Oak considered himself far superior to the humble Reed and, from a great height, looked down upon him.

"You have no pride," the Oak told the Reed. "You bend and bow to the lightest breeze. You should be more dignified. You should stand erect as I do. No wind can make me stoop or lower myself."

Just then a fierce storm sprang up. Lightning flashed and a wild gale shook the trees. The Oak stood firm for a short while. But his very stiffness was his undoing. The gale struck hard against him, tore his branches, broke his biggest boughs, and toppled him into the river. The Reed swayed and bent, letting the wind blow over him. When the storm passed he was still growing on the rim of the river.

Pride goeth before destruction,
and a haughty spirit before a fall.

The Strength of Wind and Sun

The Wind and the Sun were disputing about their strength.

"I have the strongest power that ever was," said the Sun. "Nothing can stand against me."

"Nothing except me," said the Wind. "My strength is far greater than yours."

"We shall find out," said the Sun. "I know a way to settle the argument. Do you see that Man coming down the road? Well, whichever one of us makes him take off his coat, he must be reckoned the stronger. You try first."

The Sun hid himself behind a cloud while the Wind began. The Wind blew. The Man bent his head. The Wind whistled. The Man shivered. The Wind roared and raged and sent icy blasts against the Man. But the harder the Wind blew, the closer the Man wrapped his coat about him.

"My turn now," said the Sun as it came out from behind the cloud.

At first the Sun shone gently, and the Man unbuttoned his coat and let it hang loosely from his shoulders. Then the Sun covered the whole earth with warmth. Within a few minutes the Man was so hot he was glad to take off his coat and find a shady place.

When force fails,
gentleness often succeeds.

The Nurse and the Wolf

Roaming through the countryside, a hungry Wolf was looking for something to eat. As he passed a cottage, he heard a Nurse scolding a crying child.

"Hush now," said the Nurse. "Be quiet! The next time you make that noise I'll throw you to the Wolves!"

"I seem to be in luck," thought the Wolf, licking his lips. "All I have to do is to wait a bit. The child has stopped crying, but it won't be long before it begins again. Then I can be sure of a nice juicy supper."

He did not have to wait. The child started to cry again, and the Wolf trotted briskly up to the window, wagging his tail. But when the Nurse saw the Wolf's open jaw, his red tongue and huge teeth, she shrieked.

"Go away, you horrid monster," she screamed at him, and hugged the child to her breast. "How dare you come around here! Go away, or I'll have someone shoot you!"

"Ah," said the disappointed Wolf, slinking off to the woods, "you can't trust anyone nowadays."

Don't believe everything you hear.

The Crow and the Pitcher

Dying of thirst, a Crow suddenly gave a cry of pleasure.

"Caw! Caw!" he cried. "A pitcher! A pitcher of water!"

It was indeed a pitcher, and there was water in it. But it was a large pitcher, and the water left in it was at the very bottom. The Crow could not reach down far enough to get a single sip.

"Perhaps," he said to himself, "if I push it over, the water would lie on the side and I would have no trouble getting a drink."

But the pitcher was heavy and the Crow was not able to move it at all. He was just about to give up when he thought of something which showed what a clever Crow he was.

He took a pebble from the garden, carried it in his beak, and dropped it in the pitcher. The level of the water rose a little. Then he brought another pebble and dropped that one in, too. The water rose higher. Then he brought another, and the water rose to the top of the pitcher.

With a happy gurgle, he planted his claws firmly on the rim of the pitcher and had one of the best drinks a Crow had ever had in his whole life.

Never give up. There's always a way.

I wish my beak were longer.

I wish that I were stronger.

I know what to do...find a stone or two.

Here is one.
It's pink.

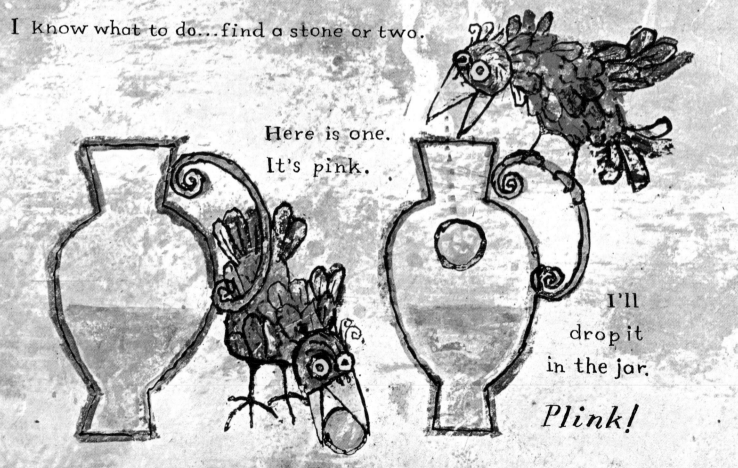

I'll
drop it
in the jar.

Plink!

Here is a nice orange stone. In you drop...

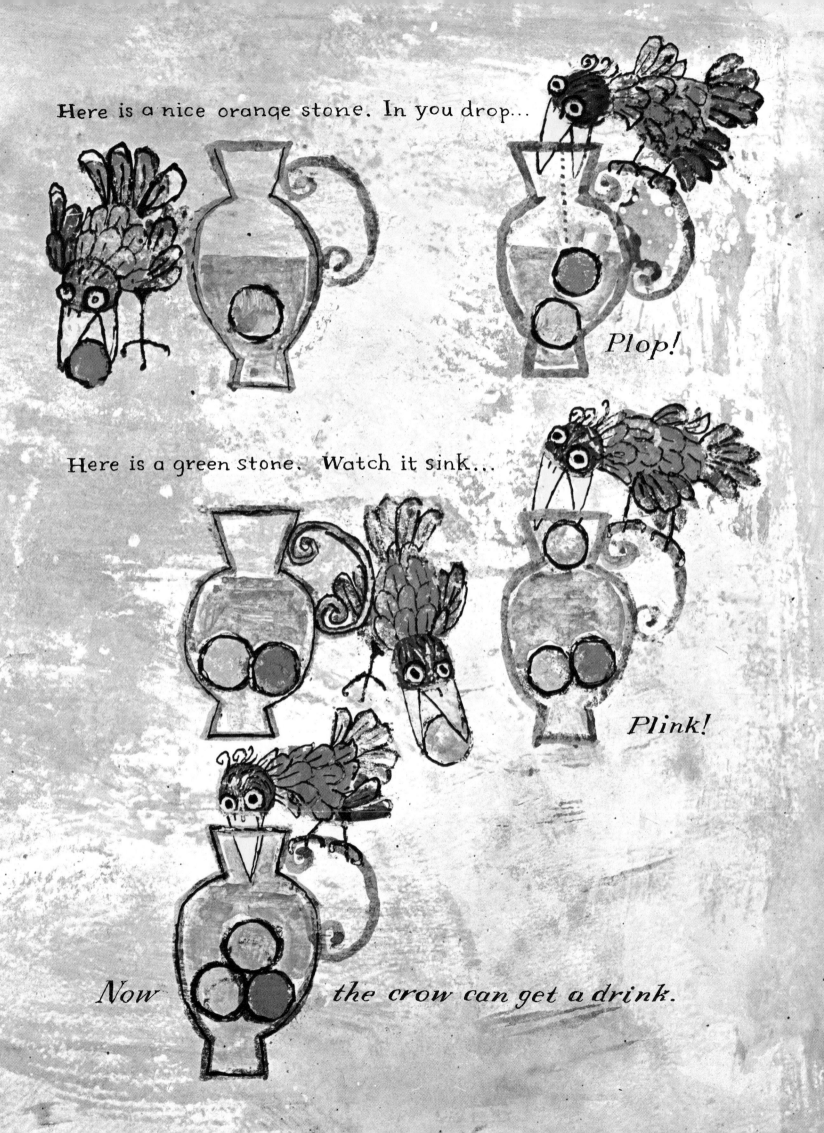

Plop!

Here is a green stone. Watch it sink...

Plink!

Now   *the crow can get a drink.*

The Boastful Bullfrog and the Bull

A Bullfrog lived in a little bog. He thought himself not only the biggest thing in the pond but the biggest thing in the world.

"I am not like other frogs," he told anyone who would listen. "I am the biggest thing of its kind. That's why they call me a Bullfrog. I am to other frogs what a Bull is to little calves."

He had heard about Bulls, but he had really never seen one. Then one day an enormous Bull came down to the pond for a drink. For a moment the Bullfrog was startled, but it did not take long before he was as conceited as ever.

"You think you're big, don't you?" he said to the Bull. "Well, I can make myself just as big as you."

The Bull said nothing. He barely looked at the croaking creature.

"You don't believe it?" said the Bullfrog. "Just you watch!"

He blew himself up to twice his size. The Bull still ignored him.

"Not big enough?" croaked the Bullfrog. "I can make myself still bigger. See!"

This time the Bull made a scornful sound and turned his head away.

This was too much for the Bullfrog. He took a huge breath and blew, and blew, and blew himself up—until he burst.

Don't try to seem bigger than you really are.

The Lions and the Hares

One day all the animals were called together. There was to be a meeting and many speeches were going to be made. A Hare spoke first.

"We Hares have not been treated fairly," he said. "Just because we are not as large as others is no reason why we shouldn't be treated as equals. We want justice. We demand our rights, and we mean to get them. Our motto is 'Share and share alike.'"

The smaller animals clapped and cheered. The larger animals said nothing but looked at the Lions. Then one of the Lions spoke.

"That was a fine speech, Mr. Hare," said the Lion. "A fine speech. But it lacks something. It lacks what Lions have and what Hares will have to get before they can expect to share with us. It lacks claws—long, sharp claws—and teeth, long sharp teeth."

And, with a roar, he bared his savage teeth and put out his cruel, knife-like claws. The Hare did not stop to argue. He ran away.

Actions speak louder than words.

UNFAIR TO HARE.
WE WANT JUSTICE AND DESSERT.
LETTUCE UNITE! WE WANT WHAT'S COMING TO US.
THE BILL OF FARE MUST BE CHANGED.

The Cunning Cat and His Company

The Cat was nine years old. To celebrate his birthday he sent out invitations to all his neighbours.

Everyone was glad to go. Next Monday at five o'clock in the afternoon, the Cat's neighbours began arriving. By half-past five the room was full. There were all sorts of birds: robins and sparrows and swallows and woodpeckers and warblers. There were fluffytail rabbits and brown bunnies. There were squirrels and chipmunks and other small beasts and birds.

"Welcome," said the Cat. "It promises to be a wonderful party. I can't tell you how pleased I am to see you all. Make yourselves at home."

"Thank you," they said. "But where's the entertainment?"

"You," said the Cat, smiling. "I expect you to entertain your-selves as well as me."

They were somewhat surprised, but they did not want to dis-please the Cat. So the birds chirped, sang their latest songs, circled in mid-air, dived from the ceiling, and looped around the room. The rabbits played leap-frog; the squirrels and chip-munks made up a game of hide-and-seek. Then they grew tired. They also grew hungry.

"And now," they said, "where's the dinner?"

"You again," said the Cat, locking the door. "You are the dinner." And, one by one, he began to eat the guests.

Next morning all that was left of the Cat's party was a large heap of fur and feathers.

Don't put your trust in fancy promises.

Cat requests the honour of your presence at the Celebration of his Birthday on Monday at five. There will be Entertainment and Dinner R.S.V.P.

The Wolf in Sheep's Clothing

A Wolf thought of a way to get his food without any trouble..

"Instead of chasing after something to eat or being chased away by dogs or men," he thought, "I will disguise myself. I will mingle with the sheep and fool the shepherd, who will think I am part of the flock. Then I can eat my fill whenever I want. All I need to do is to look like a sheep. That will be easy, for last night I noticed the skin of a sheep that had died in the woods."

The Wolf took the dead sheep's skin, put it over his body, fitted it carefully so that none of his shaggy brown fur showed anywhere, and joined a large flock of sheep.

It seemed that the trick was going to work. During the day a young lamb thought the Wolf in sheep's clothing was his mother and followed wherever he went. The Wolf led him into the forest and, when the shepherd was not looking, made a meal of the little creature.

"Aha," said the Wolf, "that was a good light lunch. It pays to be smart. Tonight when we're all in the pen, I'll kill one of the fat sheep and have a real dinner."

However, when the Wolf was shut up in the pen with the rest of the flock, an odd thing happened. The shepherd remembered he meant to slaughter an animal for his weekend meals. He took a large knife, went into the pen, and cut the throat of the first white-fleeced animal he found. It happened to be the Wolf.

Don't pretend to be what you're not.

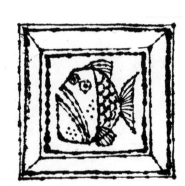 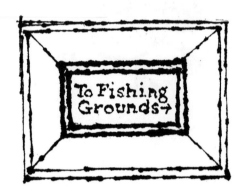

The Great and Little Fishes

"We are the terrors of the deep," said the Great Fishes. "Everything is afraid of us; we fear nothing. You, Little Fishes, do not count. You cannot fight; you are easily captured."

At that moment, the fishermen lowered a strong new net. The Great Fishes were quickly caught and hauled into the ship, while the Little Fishes escaped through the wide meshes.

It is sometimes safe to be insignificant.

A fine kettle of fish!

The Hungry Lion and the Wise Fox

The Lion was getting old, too old to hunt. Since he was no longer spry enough to get his food by force, he made up his mind to get it by cleverness. He let it be known that he was very ill and he hoped that the animals would visit him before he died.

The first to call was a Sheep. "How are you feeling today?" asked the Sheep.

"Not too well," answered the Lion. "But I'm glad you came to call."

Then a Calf came to the cave and stayed. Then a Goat paid his respects. Then a Deer and a Donkey and a pair of Rabbits. After each visit the Lion felt better; he licked his lips. All the animals of field and forest came to the royal den—all except one. The absence of the Fox annoyed the Lion, so he sent word summoning the Fox.

The Fox came, but he remained outside the Lion's cave. Standing a few feet from the opening, he said, "I hope your Majesty is feeling better now that he has had so many visitors."

"A little better, perhaps," said the Lion. "At the same time I feel bad that you have stayed away. But I won't complain. Now that you are here, come in and wish me well."

"I wish you all the health in the world," replied the Fox. "But I wish it from here. I would rather not get too close."

"And why not?" said the Lion, in his most purring voice. "Others have come in to be at my side."

"I know that," said the Fox. "And I also know something else. I notice that all the footprints of the other animals point into the cave. But I do not notice any of them pointing *out*. When some of those who came come out, I will come in. But not until then. Meanwhile, stay well—and I will, too."

Be wise, and let who can be clever.

The Fox and the Mask

A Fox who had lost his way in the city somehow got into the house of an actor. Prowling among costumes and other properties, he knocked over something.

At first it frightened him—the face was so lifelike, the forehead so firm, the mouth so threatening. Then the Fox realized it was only a mask, something that actors used to conceal their own features.

"You are a fine-looking head," said the Fox, picking it up. "A fine head indeed. It's a pity you haven't any brains."

There's nothing emptier
than an empty head.

The Hare and the Tortoise

A Hare was always boasting about his speed and sneering at a Tortoise because he was so slow. One day the Tortoise said, "You may laugh at me, but if we ever had a race I know I could beat you." "Ridiculous!" said the Hare. "Is it?" said the Tortoise. "We shall see. Are you ready?"

They started up at once and, of course, the Hare quickly outran the Tortoise who merely crawled along. The Hare, in fact, was so far ahead that he treated the whole matter as a joke and lay down. "I'll take a little nap here in the grass," he said to himself, "and when I wake up I'll finish the race far ahead."

Nevertheless, the Hare overslept himself and when he arrived at the finish line, the Tortoise, who had plodded steadily along, was there ahead of him.

The race is not always to the swift;
slow and steady is sure to win.

I wouldn't have thought it possible.

HURRAH!

STRANGE!

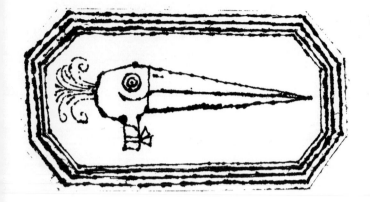

The Tricky Fox and the Stork

There was a time when the Fox and the Stork were quite good friends. It was a queer kind of friendship, for the Fox was always playing tricks on the Stork. One day he invited the Stork to dine with him. At dinnertime he placed before his guest nothing but soup in a shallow dish.

"Delicious, isn't it?" said the Fox, lapping up the soup and smacking his lips.

The Stork said nothing. Her long bill could not bring up any of the soup, so she sat there while the Fox drank and said, "Soup is my favourite food. Too bad you don't like it." The Stork did not reply for a while. But she was thinking. At last she spoke.

"I don't seem to be hungry tonight," she said when the Fox had finished. "But I would like you to return the visit. Tomorrow night I hope you will come and dine with me."

The next night when the Fox came to the Stork's house, he sniffed eagerly. Whatever the Stork was going to offer him smelled wonderful. But when the Stork brought it to the table, it was served in a long, thin jar with a very narrow mouth.

"Delicious, isn't it?" said the Stork, dipping her bill into the jar and bringing up one juicy morsel after another.

The Fox said nothing. He could not get his jaw into the narrow opening and could do nothing more than lick the outside of the vessel. The joke, he realized, was on him.

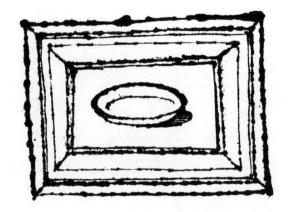

One good turn deserves another. So does a bad turn.

The Miller, the Son, and the Donkey

One day a Miller and his Son were driving their Donkey to market. They had not gone far when some girls saw them and broke out laughing. "Look!" cried one. "Look at those fools! How silly they are to be trudging along on foot when the Donkey might be carrying one of them on his back."

This seemed to make sense, so the Father lifted his Son on the Donkey and walked along contentedly by his side. They trod on for a while until they met some women who spoke to the Son scornfully. "You should be ashamed of yourself, you lazy rascal. What do you mean by riding when your poor old Father has to walk? It shows that no one respects age any more. The least you can do is get down and let your Father rest his old bones."

Red with shame, the Son dismounted and made his Father get on the Donkey's back.

They had gone only a little further when they met a group of young fellows who mocked them. "What a cruel old Man!" jeered one of the fellows. "There he sits, selfish and comfortable, while the poor Boy has to stumble along the dusty road to keep up with him."

So the Father lifted the Son up, and the two of them rode along.

However, before they reached the market place, a townsman stopped them. "Have you no feeling for dumb creatures?" he shouted. "The way that you load that little animal is a crime. You two men are better able to carry the poor little beast than he you!"

Wanting to do the right thing, the Miller and his Son got off the Donkey, tied his legs together, slung him on a pole, and carried him on their shoulders. When the crowd saw this spectacle the people laughed so loudly that the Donkey was frightened, kicked through the cords that bound him and, falling off the pole, fell into the river and was drowned.

He who tries to please everybody pleases nobody.

Boy! Let your father ride!

Now what are they doing!